GOODBYE SARAH

BY GEOFFRY BILSON

ILLUSTRATED BY RON BERG

KIDS CAN PRESS • TORONTO

This publication was produced with the generous assistance of the Canada Council, the Ontario Arts Council and the Gladys and Merrill Muttart Foundation.

Canadian Cataloguing in Publication Data

Bilson, Geoffrey, 1938-1987
    Goodbye Sarah

ISBN 0-919964-38-9

1. Winnipeg (Man.) - General Strike, 1919 - Juvenile fiction.
I. Title. II. Series.

PS8553.I47G66   jC813'.54   C82-094125-5
PZ7.B44Go

Kids Can Press Ltd.
585½ Bloor Street West
Toronto, Ontario, Canada
M6G 1K5

Cover design by Dreadnaught Design
Printed and bound in Canada by Webcom Limited

81 0 9 8 7 6 5 4

For Kate and her friend Gipsy

ONE

"I HATE him," I screamed. "I hate him, I hate him, I hate him."

Mother stopped setting the table when I burst into the kitchen. She caught me in her arms. "What's the matter Mary? Who are you hating so much?"

"Mr. Wright. I hate him. And I hate Ben and Joe, too. I hate them all. They're always picking on me."

"Slow down, dear, and tell me what happened." Mother motioned for me to sit with her at the kitchen table. She wiped the tears from my cheeks.

"Sarah and I were playing in her room with Gipsy and she wanted me to stay on because we were having fun. She asked her father if I could have supper with them, but Mr. Wright didn't even answer. He just looked at me and said, 'How's the little Bolshie today?'

"I didn't know what he was talking about. He started to laugh and they were all staring at me. Then Ben said I was blushing and Mr. Wright said that was because red was the right colour for a Communist.

"Joe and Ben were laughing so hard that they almost fell off their chairs. My face must have been bright red, then, and I ran out of the house as fast as I could. I forgot my school books but Sarah brought them out to me. I could still hear Mr. Wright and the boys laughing as I ran home."

For a few minutes mother didn't say anything. When she did speak, her voice was quiet and calm.

"Don't pay any attention to him, Mary. It's just Mr. Wright's way. He thinks the Communists are behind the strike and that all the strikers are Communist."

"But what's that got to do with me?" I asked.

"It has nothing to do with you. It's just that Mr. Wright thinks the strikers want to take over Winnipeg the way the Bolsheviks took over Russia during the Revolution. Since your father is on strike, Mr. Wright thinks that we are Communists."

"That's stupid, mother. Father doesn't want to take over Winnipeg, and neither do I."

Mother laughed. "You're right, Mary. All your father wants is a fair day's wage for a fair day's work. He works hard, but with everything costing so much, he doesn't make enough to pay for food, clothes, and rent besides. Something has to be done."

Mother hugged me. "Go and wash your face. It will make you feel better. Father will be at a strike meeting tonight, so it's just the three of us for supper."

Mr. Wright didn't seem important any more.

My brother Sam met me at the top of the stairs. "What happened?" he asked. "Why were you crying?"

"Sarah's father was making fun of me. It's no fun playing there when he's home. I wish he had never come back from the war."

"But you don't wish that father had never come home, do you?" Sam asked.

"Of course not," I said. "Father's different. He's not mean."

"Do you remember when mother told us he was coming home?" Sam asked, following me into our bedroom.

"Sure," I laughed. "You wanted me to sleep on the living room couch so we wouldn't have to share a room."

"But do you remember when he first came home?" Sam persisted. "How strange it was, everyone acting like strangers."

"All we had was the photograph that mother kept in her room to remind us what he looked like," I said. "It's no wonder we were like strangers. You were only four when he went away."

"Well you were only five," Sam added quickly, to remind me that I wasn't much older than him.

"I liked it before father got his job," Sam went on. "It was nice that he was here all the time, and we could go to the park with him and meet the other soldiers."

"He's not working now," I reminded Sam.

"But this is different. He's always at strike meetings, and he's not in as good a mood as he was then."

"He's sure in a better mood than Mr. Wright," I thought to myself.

I didn't really understand why the strike bothered Mr. Wright so much. He wasn't on strike. Every day he went to his job at the Manitoba Club dressed in a silly uniform that father said made him look like the organ grinder's monkey.

Sam and I went downstairs for supper. I did feel better, although I wished father was there. It was too much like it had been during the war with just the three of us having soup.

When Sarah and I met for school the next morning, neither of us mentioned what had happened. I didn't want to talk about it and, as it

8

turned out, neither did she. We had been best friends since grade one, and it seemed like we had always shared everything. But at that moment we could not share our thoughts.

The day went by more quickly than usual, and before I knew it, it was time to go. Sarah waited while I collected my books and then we started for home. As we reached the corner of our street, we could see Joe and Ben playing ball in her front yard.

"Come inside. I don't want to be around them," Sarah said, as if she had read my mind.

Sarah had her own room and we always played there after school.

We had just settled down on Sarah's bed when Mrs. Wright called upstairs to us, "Girls, what are you doing inside on a day like today. It's too beautiful to stay inside."

"Let's go up to the treehouse," Sarah suggested. "No one will bother us there."

The treehouse was our special place. Joe and Ben had built it, but they were too big now, and Sarah and I had taken it over.

We climbed the tree and found Gipsy napping in the shade. Sarah picked up the cat and put her on her lap. Gipsy twitched her tail, then settled down and began to purr noisily.

"I hope my father doesn't come home for supper tonight," Sarah said.

I knew I wouldn't want him to come home either if he were my father, but I still asked, "Why not?"

"He's always in a bad mood these days, going on about something or other. Right now it's the strike. It used to be that I didn't sit up straight. Is your father like that?"

"Not really. He talks about the strike too, but mostly he tells us stories."

"About the war?" asked Sarah.

I thought for a moment. "No. He doesn't talk about the war at all. He says it's best forgotten."

"That's all my father talks about," said Sarah. "I can't stand it, but Ben and Joe love it. He's always talking about rats in the trenches, and machine gun nests and people being caught on barbed wire and then shot. He just goes on and on."

Sarah sounded as though she was going to cry. I guess we were both thinking about our fathers, because we were quiet for a few minutes. Suddenly, Sarah started to laugh.

"Did I tell you, I've decided to go on the stage?" she said. "I want to be a famous actress and travel all around Canada and maybe to London and Paris, too."

"But I'll never see you again if you do that," I said.

"Sure you will. You'll be my manager. We'll travel together."

It seemed like a good idea to me. We had almost finished planning our trip when Mrs. Wright called Sarah for supper.

"I have to go now," I said quickly. I didn't want Sarah to ask her father if I could eat with them.

That was what had started the problems the day before.

"Okay," said Sarah, "See you tomorrow."

That night, there was soup and bread again for supper; thin soup and dark bread. Sam complained through the whole meal that he was being starved, but he got his fair share. Every time we sat down to eat, we hoped that the strike would end soon.

Father was at another strike meeting and it wasn't until we had almost finished that he came storming into the house.

"Liz, Liz have you heard the news yet?" father shouted before he reached the kitchen. "Better things are on their way. This is a big day for the union."

He pulled up a chair to the table and wrapped his arm around Sam's shoulder. "We'll win our strike now. All the workers are going to join us. It's to be a general strike. We can't lose!"

"You're not a general," Sam said. "You told me you were a corporal."

Father and mother both laughed.

"Nothing to do with generals, Sammy. It means other workers are going to join the metal workers' strike. Streetcar drivers, railway workers, office clerks, they're all going out. Winnipeg is going to be shut down."

"Teachers too?" I asked hopefully.

"No, Mary. But if everyone else goes out — all

the workers together — we'll have one big union. Then the bosses will have to talk sense and soon we'll be back at work with enough pay for us to eat meat every night and for you and Sammy to wear velvet."

"I hate velvet," Sam said, looking disappointed.

I knew that father was exaggerating but it felt nice to see him so excited and happy.

We finished dinner and Sam and I went upstairs to do our homework. We could hear mother and father talking in the kitchen long after we were supposed to be asleep.

"I hope the strike ends soon," I said to Sam.

"It's sure to now. If everyone goes on strike it'll have to be over very soon." Sam sounded so sure.

TWO

WHEN we came down to breakfast the next morning all that was on the table was the teapot.

"What's this, mother?" father asked.

"Tea!" Mother's voice was tense. "Ken, the money won't stretch any more. I can make the children lunch and give us some supper but until the strike ends, it's tea for breakfast."

"I'll starve," Sam wailed. "I know I'll die." He pushed the cup of black tea away. "I'm not going to drink it."

"You will, Sam," father said in a tone he hadn't used before. "I'll not have you going to school with nothing in your belly."

Sam muttered to himself, but he drank the tea. I wished we could have milk in it, but we hadn't had milk in the house for a while.

Mother said we just couldn't afford it. But that didn't stop her from going to the window each morning to watch for the milkman.

"Mr. Johanson's late today," she commented, "Mr. Wright is outside looking angry."

"He's not late. He'll not be coming at all," father grinned. "The milkmen have joined the strike, too. I think I'll go over and tell Bob Wright that."

We all looked at father with surprise. I followed him outside and watched as he walked next door to the Wright's house.

I couldn't make out what the men were saying to each other until Mr. Wright started to shout. "Is that what your general strike means, Jarrett? You'll start by starving the children of their milk! Fine men you must be to pick on children."

"Talk sense, man," father shouted back. "No children will starve because the milkman doesn't call. But there are plenty of children of milkmen and other workers starving because their fathers can't earn a living wage by their work."

The two men were so close together, with their red faces and angry words that I was sure they would start to fight.

"Father, father, mother says to come to breakfast," I called.

Father turned away from Mr. Wright and came towards me. I could see Sarah's father glaring at me angrily before he stormed into his own house.

"Breakfast, eh lass," father laughed, running his hand over my head. "Were you afraid I'd attack Sergeant Bob on his own doorstep?"

I didn't answer, but held his hand tightly until we were in the house.

THREE

"WHAT was going on this morning?" Sarah
asked when we met to go to school. "Father was
really angry. He said a lot of things about
Bolshies and revolution and starving children. I'm
not starving! I don't know what he was on about.
Then, he got really mad when mother reminded
him that he had to leave for work early because
the streetcars weren't running." Sarah giggled,
"You should have seen him. He got so red I
thought he would burst."

I knew what she meant. I almost wished he
would burst, but I didn't say so.

When we got to school, Ben and Joe and some
of their friends were waiting at the gate. They
pointed at me and began chanting, "Bolshie,
Bolshie."

Ben snatched the tam off my head.

"Stop it Ben," Sarah said, and she pushed him away, while I grabbed my tam. "Leave Mary alone."

"What do you want with her anyway, Sarah," Ben said angrily. "Dad told you to keep away from her."

"Stop it!" Sarah shouted. "I don't know what you mean. Mary's my friend."

"You ought to leave her alone, Sarah. Dad won't like it if you don't," Joe added.

"I don't care." Sarah grabbed my arm and pulled me through the groups of boys into the school yard. I could see Sam watching us. I knew that if he tried to come to my rescue there would be a fight.

Luckily, Mr. Porter came out to ring the bell and the boys hurried to their entrance while we went to ours. Some of the girls stared at us and whispered, but no one said anything directly.

We always began the day by singing *God Save the King* and *The Maple Leaf Forever*. Then we would sit, hands folded on our desks, until Miss Wilson began the lesson.

Miss Wilson's grey hair was very carefully brushed. There was never a strand out of place. Her high necked blouse was fastened at the throat with a large broach, and she always wore a plain grey skirt.

I imagined that she had a whole closet full of plain grey skirts but Sarah said she only had one.

"It's a special material," Sarah teased. "She sleeps in it at night but it never gets creased. As soon as she wakes up, she's ready for school."

I almost believed it because Miss Wilson was so strict and rigid in her routine.

"Quiet children!" she called, banging on the desk for silence with her long wooden pointer. "You are here to work. There is no substitute for honest, hard work. It always brings a fair reward. Now, take out your readers."

I stole a glance at Sarah who rolled her eyes toward the ceiling and made such a funny face that I started to laugh.

"I would not expect you to believe that Mary Jarrett," Miss Wilson snapped. "I do, however, expect you to pay attention when you are in my classroom. We can only hope that here you will acquire good working habits."

Her pets giggled — all except Sarah. They always did when she said nasty things to the children she disliked. I didn't know why she disliked me, but she had from the first day of school and she was growing meaner to me as the days went on.

We worked all morning on arithmetic. Miss Wilson called me to the black board to do problems. There was one I just couldn't figure out.

"Surely you know enough to carry the remainder over to here, Mary," she said. Snatching the chalk out of my hand, she made a few quick changes in the work and then erased it without explaining anything.

"If you look at Sarah's work you will see how it should be done."

I felt like crying, but I wouldn't let myself. Sarah gave me a quick smile as I passed her on the way back to my seat, but Miss Wilson was watching so Sarah couldn't say anything.

It was like that all day and I was glad when it was time to go home. At least we had a weekend free from Miss Wilson.

I didn't have much to say on the way home that afternoon. Even Sarah's imitation of Miss Wilson, with her lips pursed and her finger wagging couldn't make me laugh. She became quite cross.

"You don't have to be so miserable just because Miss Wilson was rude. She's always like that."

"She was more like it today," I said.

"That's silly, Mary," Sarah replied.

"You think everything is silly, Sarah. Well it's not! It's all right for you, you're one of her pets. But she's always getting after me and it's horrible."

By the time I finished I was nearly screaming. Sarah looked startled. I had never shouted at her like that before.

We finished walking home in silence.

"Coming in?" She asked when we got to her house. She said it quietly and did not look at me.

"No, I think I'll go home. See you tomorrow."

Sarah nodded and went inside. I watched her close the door. It was the first time since we became best friends that we hadn't played together after school.

FOUR

I DIDN'T see Sarah on Saturday. She went with her mother to her grandmother's, as they often did on the weekend. Sam and I played together for most of the day although I would have liked to spend some time alone in the treehouse. I didn't because Ben and Joe were home and I wouldn't go by myself.

Father had gone to a meeting at Victoria Park and came home late in the afternoon looking gloomy.

"What's the matter, father?" I asked him, when he sat down to watch the game of jacks that Sam and I were playing.

"You don't miss a thing, do you Mary?" he said. "They've hired scabs, now."

I was silent. I didn't know what scabs were, and I could tell by Sam's expression that he didn't know either. But I knew they were serious because mother came and sat down too. She looked very worried.

"Scabs are people hired to do the work of strikers," mother began to explain.

"It's a way that the bosses can keep things going. They're signing up scab firemen right now." Father began to sound angry. "Those fine gentlemen at the Manitoba Club mean to force us back to work. They ought to know this isn't the way to do it. People are angry."

"What will happen," Sam asked.

"Well, Sammy, it could get very difficult. The union leaders are trying to keep things calm but the men are ready to fight."

"Really fight?" I asked.

"Yes, Mary. But there must be a better way than fighting. We've all had enough fighting. Four long years in the trenches and fighting like I hope you'll never have to see. My closest friend killed just a few feet away from me. Yet, it doesn't seem to have changed things here for the better."

Father's voice was shaking, but not with anger. It was the first time he had talked about the war. Sam started to ask another question, but changed his mind. It was easy to see that it had been difficult for father to say as much as he had.

Supper was quiet that evening. No one seemed in the mood to talk. After we had finished, father went to another strike committee meeting and Sam and I were asleep before he came home.

Sunday started badly. We were getting ready for church when I heard the milk cart. I ran to the window.

"It's the milkman," I called. "The strike must be over."

"No, Mary, not yet," said father, who had joined me at the window. "The strike committee decided last night to let the milkmen go their rounds. There were so many complaints from folks like Mr. Wright who said we were trying to starve the children and babies, that we thought we would gain more support if we let the milk deliveries continue."

The milk cart had already reached the Wright's. We watched Mr. Johanson carry his milk crate up the path to where Mr. Wright stood, looking very satisfied. Mr. Johanson took two bottles from the crate and put them on the step. Father opened the window so that we could hear what was said.

"Good to see you back at work Johanson," Mr. Wright said. "You didn't let the Bolshies keep you away from your job for long, I see."

"We're not Bolshies, Wright," the milkman snapped. "I got the okay from the strike committee to go my rounds." He pointed to his wagon. There was a large sign pinned on the side which said: PERMITTED BY AUTHORITY OF THE STRIKE COMMITTEE.

Mr. Wright's face reddened with anger. "What's that?" he shouted.

"That's just so folks know that I'm no scab," Mr. Johanson said. He walked away, clucking for his horse to follow him down the road.

Mr. Wright began shouting to our neighbours who had come running to their doors when they heard the milk wagon.

"D'you see that. Now the strikers tell us who can and can't work. Before this is over honest men will be attacked in the streets for working. They're planning a revolution, I tell you. Let them get away with this and there'll be Communists here in Winnipeg. It'll be like Moscow and the Bolsheviks will be in City Hall." He was breathless by now, waving his arms and shouting, as a small crowd gathered to listen.

"I'm not standing for this," father muttered and he ran out of the house, over to Mr. Wright. Mother followed him while Sam and I stood at the door and watched.

"Come on Wright, talk sense," father shouted. "There's no revolution planned and you know it. Two days ago you said we were killing babies by stopping the milkmen, now we let them work and you say it's revolution."

24

"Just listen to yourself, Jarrett," Mr. Wright shouted back. "Who are you to say who can and can't work here. You don't run this city yet and I tell you straight, you and your sort won't run it while I'm around to stop you." His neck swelled against his collar and his eyes began to bulge.

"My sort? What is my sort, Wright? Just workmen and old soldiers like yourself, trying to make a living for our families."

"You know better than that, Jarrett. You're being used man. If you're not a revolutionary then you're a fool."

The crowd began to shift and murmur, and someone shouted, "Why don't you give him one, Jarrett?"

I was sure that this time father would hit Mr. Wright. I had never seen him look so angry. Mr. Wright, with his fists already clenched, was ready for a fight.

Suddenly, mother and Mrs. Wright pushed between the men. As they did, father and Mr. Wright stepped back.

"We've sworn to keep this strike peaceful, Wright, and that's how we'll keep it while we can. But if you push us too far, I'll not answer for all our men."

He turned and walked back to the house with mother. I could see that Sam was nearly crying.

"It's all right, Sam, father isn't hurt."

"He should have hit him. Why didn't he?" His

voice was full of anger. He ran upstairs before I could answer.

It was then that I saw Sarah, standing in her yard, watching me.

I ran over to her. "Sarah, I hate all this arguing and meanness. Why do they have to do it?" I reached over to her and gave her a hug, but she just stood there.

"Your father was going to hit my father," she said.

I let go of her, not knowing what to say.

"Well, your father looked ready to hit mine, too," I said quietly.

Sarah turned away without another word and walked to her house. The door closed behind her and I was left alone, standing on the path between our houses.

FIVE

MONDAY morning, Sarah was waiting for me. Joe and Ben were waiting with her. I could feel myself blushing as I walked towards them.

"Come on Sarah," Joe said. "You don't want to walk with her."

"Yeah, Sarah. We'll walk you to school today," echoed Ben.

"Stop it," Sarah demanded. "Mary's my friend and we always walk to school together. We'll go together today, too."

Sarah said it so firmly that her brothers walked away, but not without first giving me a dirty look.

"I thought you asked them to wait with you," I said to her after the boys had left.

"Of course not," she said.

At that moment, things between us seemed the way they had always been. "I was worried all day yesterday about what happened," I said.

"You should have heard my father after he came in," Sarah exclaimed. "I was sure he would hit one of us, he was so mad. He was shouting about revolution in the streets and stupid men being used and how the army should be brought in to shoot the strike committee. It was awful. Even mother couldn't calm him down. I don't know why he didn't hit your father either, he was so mad."

"Sam asked my father why he didn't fight, too. But father said he had had four years of fighting in the war and that was enough."

"I wish everyone would talk about something other than strikes and war. I'm so tired of hearing it," Sarah said with a sigh.

"If only everyone wasn't so angry or sad all the time."

"Look, there's Minnie, and she's wearing those silly boots. She thinks she's so fancy in them. Let's catch up to her," Sarah said, hurrying down the road.

I knew it was her way of changing the subject but I was happy to follow after her.

Miss Wilson made us sing *Rule Brittania* and *God Save the King*, before class began.

"These are difficult times, children. Our city is being threatened by foreign ideas and foreign people. Perhaps some of you saw the milk carts this weekend, and realized that a small body of men have taken it upon themselves to decide who can and who cannot work. Our newspapers have been shut by these same people and no news can be printed. I am certain, however, that in time, law and order will be restored. Winnipeg will not slide into anarchy."

I looked at Sarah, who raised her eyebrows at me and made her eyes very big. I had never heard Miss Wilson sound so angry before. She hadn't even noticed that the class was shuffling uncomfortably in their seats. Then, without warning, Miss Wilson banged her ruler on the desk.

"Can anyone tell me what anarchy means?" she demanded.

No one put up a hand.

"I'll tell you what it means. It means the absence of law and government. And the absence of law and government results in disorder and lawlessness. The Communists want to bring us to this condition but they will not succeed."

Her lesson finally ended and recess began. Sarah and I went to our usual spot in the girls' yard.

"Miss Wilson was really strange this morning," Sarah said. She began to imitate the teacher standing rigidly in front of the class, banging her ruler and shaking her finger at us.

I loved it when Sarah acted. Her imitations

made me laugh until my sides felt like they might split.

She probably would have continued until the bell rang if it hadn't been for a terrible ruckus that broke out in the boys' yard. Everyone ran over to see what was happening.

I couldn't believe it when I saw Sam at the front of a gang of boys who were shouting, "Scabs, scabs, your fathers are all scabs."

They were jeering and shaking their fists at the other gang who were marching toward them chanting, "Bolshie, Bolshie, go home Bolshies."

The boys were moving closer and closer to each other and as Sarah and I watched, the two gangs began to fight.

"Look at those stupid boys," Sarah said. "They're always fighting about something."

The recess teacher, Mr. Porter, heard the commotion and came racing over. He managed to separate the boys and stop the fighting just as the bell rang. But from then on, every chance they got, the gangs would form.

"It's just like in town," Sam said. "The strikers march and the people against the strikers march, and everyone yells things at everyone else."

"But the strikers don't fight," I reminded him.

Sam just grinned at me.

SIX

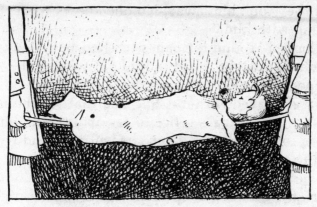

AS the days grew hotter, our classroom got
stuffier and smellier. Everyone waited for the
summer holidays to begin. Some of the other
children had even stopped coming to school
because of the strike, but mother insisted that
Sam and I go.

We had gotten used to having only tea for
breakfast, but we couldn't get used to the fact
that supper was becoming smaller and smaller.

I was luckier than Sam. At lunch, Sarah always
shared her meal with me. She pretended that she
was too full to finish, but I knew it wasn't true.
Sam had to make do with only the bread and
syrup mother packed for us.

One day, as I was coming out of school, some
of Sam's friends ran up to me. "Sam's been taken

to hospital; he just fell down at the blackboard and they took him away. No one knows what's wrong with him."

I looked around for Sam's teacher, but she was nowhere in sight. I had to find out what had happened to my brother.

Sarah stayed with me. She said that we should go to the principal's office to ask about Sam, but I was too frightened. Then the bell rang and we had to return to our classroom.

The afternoon went very slowly. I couldn't work for thinking about Sam. Sarah kept turning toward me during history class to make sure I was okay and once she reached across the aisle to hold my hand.

"Mary Jarrett, come up here." Miss Wilson's voice was very shrill. "And you too Sarah. I want to see the note."

Sarah and I looked at each other blankly. "What note, Miss Wilson?" I asked.

"Don't be impudent, Mary. I saw you passing a note."

"No, Miss Wilson we were just ..." Sarah came to my rescue, but Miss Wilson didn't let her finish.

"I cannot believe that. If you deny passing a note, then I can only believe that you are lying."

Miss Wilson sent us both to the principal with her own note about what she thought we had done. By the time we got to the office, I was crying and Sarah, with her arm around my shoulder, was crying too.

Mr. Rounthwaithe called us in. Sarah handed him Miss Wilson's note.

"Mary Jarrett, your brother was taken to hospital today, as you know. We don't think it's serious, but it has obviously upset you so you may go home early. Sarah, you go with her and see that she gets home all right."

I couldn't believe that we were going to get off without a scolding.

"But mind, girls," Mr. Rounthwaite continued, "don't think this means that we will permit rudeness or insolent behaviour. Next time you are rude to your teacher, you will have to answer for it."

Despite the heat, Sarah and I ran all the way home and raced into the house. Mother was sitting at the kitchen table with a glass of water. She looked hot, and I could tell she had been crying.

"What's wrong with Sam?" we asked.

"Nothing girls." Mother's voice was tense. "The doctor said he'll be fine in a few days. Aren't you home early?"

"Does he have to have an operation?" Sarah asked.

"There's nothing wrong with Sam," mother said quickly.

She wouldn't say anything else while Sarah was there.

That evening, at supper, as we sat drinking

our soup, mother began to cry quietly just as she used to do during the war when reading father's letters.

"There now, mother, the doctor said Sam will be fine," father tried to console her.

"Oh, Ken, I'm so worried. The doctor says Sam's malnourished. They're keeping him in the hospital to feed him, to build up his strength. The child's starving, Ken! How can we have let that happen? For God's sake, isn't there some way to stop this. The doctor said the strike is starving the children. Why don't you all just stop it!" Her voice grew louder and louder.

"Easy now, mother. It's not the strike that's starving the children. It's the little money we bring home when we're working that's starving the children. Something has got to change."

"I don't care," mother snapped. "All I know is there's no money coming in. Look around. Our winter clothes are in the pawn shop, we've sold so much of our furniture. The pawn shop has near everything we own. There's nothing left to borrow on, Sam's starving and you've only to look at Mary to see what's becoming of her. I don't know where we'll get the rent money next week."

Mother went upstairs and shut her door. There was nothing father could say. We sat silently for a time, drinking our tea.

"What did mother mean about the rent?" I finally asked.

"Don't worry about it, Mary. It'll all come

34

right," father said briskly.

"But if we can't pay the rent, what will happen?"

"Mary, we'll have to leave here. One of the neighbours has been complaining about us to the rentman, and I don't think we'll get credit much longer."

I could tell from father's tone which of the neighbours he meant.

"But we can't leave." I said.

Father stared into his empty cup. "It's no good. We need a bit of action or this whole strike will fail. Children are starving and people are breaking down under the strain of it all. That's not what we were looking for. You get yourself to bed, Mary, I've a meeting to go to. Something has to be done about all this."

I couldn't sleep that night. At last, just like Sarah, I had a room to myself, but this wasn't how I had wanted it to be. It seemed too quiet and empty without Sam. I was used to him snoring and thrashing around and now it felt lonely lying there alone. There was so much to think about too, especially what father had said about leaving. We were already behind in the rent. How could that be! No credit and we would have to leave. Leave the house and leave Sarah. I wished with all my might that father would be working when I woke up in the morning, but I knew it wouldn't happen.

SEVEN

"WHAT'S wrong with Sam, anyway?" Sarah
asked me as we walked to school the next day.

"Nothing! He just has to stay in hospital for a
few more days."

I couldn't look at Sarah as we spoke. I knew
that mother didn't want me to talk about Sam to
anyone, and how could I say that he was
starving? It wasn't our fault that we had so little
food, but somehow I felt guilty.

"Why would he have to stay if there's nothing
wrong?" Sarah persisted.

"I don't know," I said firmly. "It's nothing."

"Oh well, if you don't want to tell me, I don't
care." Sarah bristled.

I could tell that she was hurt, but I couldn't let
mother down. We walked on in silence.

Sam came home after five days. He looked better, not as pale as before. It was almost impossible to get him to stop talking about the hospital and what he had to eat there.

"We had milk with every meal, and meat and cheese and lots of bread," he told us enthusiastically.

I knew he wasn't bragging or trying to make anyone feel bad, but I could tell that mother was upset and I simply felt hungry.

"This has gone on too long. I'm going to get some work," mother said. "I'm not having my children drop down half-starved in school."

Mother was a good seamstress and during the war she had worked for several rich families in Winnipeg, mending clothes and making new ones. Now she set off to see her old employers and ask for work. It meant long walks through the hot streets. She looked tired and angry when she came home that first night.

"It's unbelievable Mary, the rudeness I've met today. People I've sewn for; people who've known me for years, shut the door in my face. They asked if father is a striker and then just slammed the door."

"But father's not doing the sewing, you are," I said.

"Some of them are frightened, Mary. They won't even let me in their houses. It's as if I have the plague."

Mother did find some sewing to do and made a little money to help out. But not very many people would hire a striker's wife and some who did, tried to pay her less than she had been paid during the war.

Father was spending even more time working with the strike committee. He was helping to organize parades and meetings, trying to win support for the strike. The people against the strike had also begun organizing parades. There was a lot of shouting and name-calling whenever the strikers and the non-strikers were near each other. It was like the boys' schoolyard at recess, only there were no teachers to break up the arguments.

Mother was worried that there would be a fight between the two groups of men and since father was with the demonstrations almost all the time now, I know she thought that he would get hurt.

The mayor was also beginning to worry that people would get hurt, and as father said, took action. No one was allowed to demonstrate for the strike or against it. He must have thought that would help things to calm down, but it didn't. Instead, things worsened, and as they did, we saw less and less of father.

One evening, just as mother, Sam and I were

sitting down to supper, father came into the house.

"They've fired the regular policemen, and now they're hiring scabs in their place." He sat down at the table and rested his head in his hands for a moment. "Wright is one of them. I might have guessed that he would join sometime. They'll use the scabs to break the strike for sure."

We sat in silence as father described what had been going on downtown all day.

"Mary, I want you to keep away from the Wrights. All of them!" father demanded.

I couldn't believe it. "But Sarah's my friend," was all I could say.

"I don't care. I don't want you around that scab's house or with anyone related to him."

"Ken, please," mother came to my rescue. "They're only children. Isn't this bad enough without involving them further?"

But father insisted. "This strike is for all of us, mother. If it fails, we all lose."

The tears welled in my eyes, and I couldn't hold them back.

"I don't care what you say, I'm going to play with Sarah," I shouted as I pushed away from the table and ran upstairs.

EIGHT

SARAH and I did keep playing together, but we hardly ever played inside anymore. Mr. Wright was home so much now and even though I had told father that I would still be friends with Sarah, I knew that he would be very angry if I was in her house. So we spent most of our time in the treehouse.

One afternoon when we had nothing much to do, Sarah said, "I wish Gipsy was here. If I go inside to get her, father probably won't let me come out again. Things were so much more fun before this stupid strike began. Now father has joined some silly group called the Specials and he doesn't want me outside because he thinks there is going to be trouble. It's all so stupid."

I listened to Sarah without saying a word. I couldn't believe that all she could say about the strike was that it was stupid and silly. She sounded so stupid herself. When she started on again about how the strikers should go back to work and then everything would be all right, I couldn't listen any more.

"Some people are starving for this strike, Sarah. It's not silly or stupid. The only thing that is stupid is your father. He's a scab, don't you know that. That's what the Specials are, they're scab policemen."

We were both silent. I couldn't look at Sarah and I knew she wasn't looking at me. I wished the treehouse floor would open so that I could disappear. I wanted to go home.

Before I could do anything, I heard shouting coming from below. When I looked down I saw boys scuffling together on the sidewalk.

"What is it?" Sarah asked.

"Some boys fighting," I looked more closely. "It's Ben and Joe and ..." I screamed loudly, "Sam." And before I knew it I was scrambling down the tree.

"Leave him alone," I yelled as I raced toward the fight, with Sarah close behind me. "Leave my brother alone."

Sam was lying on the ground, blood streaming from his nose. As I got closer, Ben and Joe backed off.

"Do you always fight two against one." I glared at them both and knelt next to Sam. "And he's smaller than you, too."

I turned to Sarah. "Two against one isn't fair."

"I bet Sam started it," Sarah said. "He's always going on about scabs and starting fights."

I stood up to face her. I was so angry that I felt I could have fought with Sarah at that moment. But we just stood glaring at each other, our faces red and our fists clenched.

"If you like your brothers so much, why don't you play with them?"

Sarah's eyes filled with tears, and she turned and ran after her brothers who had walked away by this time.

I stood staring down at Sam, fighting my own tears.

"Why did you talk to Sarah like that?" he asked. "I thought she was your best friend."

"I wonder, Sam," I said. "Come on, you're bleeding. Let's go home."

NINE

ON Friday morning when I woke up, I could hear mother and father talking in the kitchen. Their voices were loud, not the way they usually spoke.

"They've been shouting like that for hours," said Sam.

We both got dressed and tiptoed downstairs to the kitchen door where we could listen.

"It's ridiculous to go on, Ken," mother was saying. "You have no hope of winning anymore, and there can only be trouble with these marches. Now you tell me they're arresting people. Where would we be if they arrested you?"

"Look, Liz, we've started this and we've got to finish. We've got to win or we'll be in a worse way than we ever were."

"Ken, your pride is getting in the way. Look at us! Tea for breakfast, Sam nearly starving, and now nowhere to live. It's pointless, I tell you, pointless."

Sam and I ran into the kitchen. Our parents turned to us wearily.

"What do you mean we have nowhere to live?" blurted Sam.

"What kind of trouble will there be because of the parades? Are they going to arrest you, father?" I asked.

"Sit down and have your tea," father said.

"But will they arrest you?" I asked again.

"They've arrested some of our men, Mary. There are hundreds of men working for the strike committee. I doubt that they will try to arrest all of us. I'm pretty small fry, but it is something that we should be prepared for, just in case."

Sam and I were frightened by the things father was saying. He seemed so calm, yet he was talking about going to jail. Like a criminal!

"There will be a big rally on Saturday to protest the arrests," father continued.

Sam and I were still thinking about father going to jail.

"Why would they put you in jail?" I persisted. "You haven't stolen anything or hurt anyone."

"These are funny times, Mary," he replied.

That wasn't much of an answer, but it was all that he would say. I hardly dared ask the other question, but I had to.

"Mother, why did you say that we have nowhere to live?"

There was a long silence, during which neither mother nor father looked at us.

"They have to know, mother."

"We're leaving here, children," mother said, her voice tight. "We've been put out. We don't have money to pay the rent and the landlord won't let us owe it another week. There have been complaints from the neighbours. So, we have to be out today."

"We can't move. I won't go. This is my house, I can't leave it. What about school and my friends."

As I spoke, I knew that what I was saying was nonsense, but it just came pouring out along with my tears.

"We know you don't want to leave, love," father said, taking me onto his knee. "Mother and I don't want to leave either, but we've no choice. We won't be going far away, so you can come visit. You'll make new friends, Mary. And just think, you won't have to see Miss Wilson again."

"It won't be the same," I sobbed.

"I'll not deny that. It seems that nothing is to be the same."

It was time for Sam and me to get ready for school, although neither of us wanted to go. Sam went on ahead, and when I came out of the house Sarah was waiting.

"Hello," she said quietly when I had reached her.

"Hello," was all I replied.

We walked to school in silence, until Sarah finally asked, "What's the matter, Mary? Are you still angry about yesterday?"

Part of me wanted to tell her the bad news, but it wouldn't come out. I just looked away.

"Nothing's the matter."

"There's got to be something. You've been crying."

My voice became firm. "It's nothing."

She began to walk more quickly and didn't look at me when she spoke.

"Well, you don't have to tell me if you don't want to. There seem to be a lot of things you won't tell me anymore."

The day dragged. Miss Wilson continued to pick on me, but somehow it didn't matter; I just didn't hear her.

Sarah and I walked home from school. We didn't say much more than we had that morning.

"I think I'll go home," I said when we arrived at her house. I didn't want to go up to the treehouse again, ever.

"Okay. See you tomorrow," she said, and she went into her house without looking back.

Mother was packing kitchen things when I walked in.

"Not playing with Sarah today, dear?" she asked.

"No, mother."

She put down the bowl she had been wrapping and looked at me.

"What's wrong, Mary? Did Sarah say something about our moving that upset you?"

"I didn't tell Sarah we were leaving. I couldn't. I knew she wouldn't understand. Mother, I don't think Sarah's going to be my friend anymore. I can't talk to her as I used to. I hate this. Everything was fine before the strike and now everything is wrong."

Mother put her arms around me.

"Some things that are worth doing are very hard, Mary. I know it doesn't seem fair that they have to be so hard."

As soon as it was dark, we began to move. We didn't have very much, because so many of our things had already been taken to the pawn shop. What was left was loaded into a handcart that father and Sam pushed down the street.

As mother shut the back door, we stopped to look at the empty kitchen. It seemed so much bigger without the table and chairs. We went upstairs to make sure nothing had been left. Then, for the first time that I could remember, we locked the front door.

"Do you want to say goodbye to Sarah, now?" mother asked.

I just shook my head. Mother and I walked down the street silently, without looking back.

We crossed the tracks leading to the railroad yards and turned on Logan Avenue where we caught up with father and Sam. The street was busy with traffic and people. We worked our way through the crowds and turned several times before coming to a short street where we stopped. There were no trees here, just small houses jammed together.

"Here we are," father said. "Sid will take us in until we get fixed up."

Sid Stein was a friend of father's, a striker who had worked for the railway. He was a widower with grown children and now lived alone.

He came out to greet us and help father and Sam move our furniture into a shed next to his house. Sid's house was even smaller than ours.

"Well I hope we don't disturb you too much," mother said as Sid showed us our room. It had a big double bed in it and some mattresses on the floor.

"Why no, Mrs. Jarrett. It'll be good to hear voices in the house again," Sid said kindly.

"It's awful, Sam," I whispered. "We've left our house and look at us now, all in one room and with hardly any of our own things."

Sam seemed not to mind at all. He went outside and found some boys playing ball on the street and in no time at all, was acting as if he'd always lived in the neighbourhood. I sat on the porch for a while and watched the boys cheering and laughing together.

That evening after we had eaten a late supper, Sid looked hard at me and with a sly smile, he said, "I think that what we need is a song."

He went to the closet and brought out a silver banjo. The banjo looked very small in his big calloused hands but the music it made was so happy and bright it filled the room. We all began to feel more cheerful.

"Here's one for you Mary. It's all about a family that has to move house. Now listen and sing the chorus with me."

He began to sing:

My old man
Said follow the van
And don't dilly dally on the way
Off went the van with my home
  packed in it
I walked behind with my old cock linnet
But I dilly'd and dally'd and dally'd
  and dilly'd

Lost my way and don't know
   where to roam
Oh you can't trust the Specials like the
   old time Coppers
When you can't find your way home.

I felt silly at first, but the tune was very catchy, and soon we were all singing along. Sid and father liked the line about the Specials so we sang that part a couple of extra times.

"You've got a real Marie Lloyd, there, Mrs. Jarrett." Sid said pointing at me. "We'll see her on the stage one day."

That reminded me of Sarah and how she was going to be an actress. It seemed a very long time ago since the talk in the treehouse about our trip and me being her manager.

I lay awake that night, thinking about Sarah. I felt terrible about having left without telling her. We had been best friends for so long, and I hadn't even said goodbye.

TEN

"WELL, Ken, are you going downtown this afternoon?" Sid asked as we ate breakfast.

Sam had to be told to be polite as he was reaching for his third piece of bread and jam, but Sid said, "Let the boy eat, he's growing."

"I think I'd better go, Sid. The committee's hoping to keep things peaceful but, with all the Specials and talk about the army coming in to stop the strike, it could get nasty again."

"It's ending, Ken, you and I know it," Sid said. "We'll not get our one big union after all. We'll not get anything out of it. I only hope things don't get too ugly."

"What's happening, father?" I asked.

"Oh, some old soldiers are going to parade at

City Hall in support of the strike. There was trouble with the Specials at the last parade and there's a chance this one could turn nasty too. You children must not go downtown this afternoon. You could get hurt."

"Do you have to go, Ken?" mother asked.

"The committee asked me to," he replied.

"What do you mean about it ending, Mr. Stein?" Sam asked.

Sid shrugged his shoulders. "Well Sammy, we can't hold out much longer. We haven't built our one big union and many of our leaders have been arrested. Now there's talk of using the army. I reckon we'll be back at work soon enough with nothing to show for it.

Sid and father got ready to go and, in spite of mother's warning, Sam and I walked with them as far as Logan Avenue. As we neared Main Street, a streetcar was just turning the corner.

"Look at that," father said, pointing as it clattered by. "They've found scabs to drive the cars. They'd better not come downtown this afternoon."

"Can't you stop them?" Sam asked.

"It'd mean a lot of trouble, but maybe that's coming," answered Sid thoughtfully.

They left us with another warning about staying near home. Sam and I spent the rest of the morning exploring the neighbourhood around Logan Avenue. There were many small side streets leading to the railway tracks and we seemed to go up and down them all. Finally, we found our way back to Main Street and watched the crowds hurrying towards City Hall.

"It's going to be a big show," Sam said. "Look at those people."

Some of the men who passed were wearing their old army uniforms but most were wearing ordinary clothes. Entire families went by.

Sam was all for joining the crowds, and I began to worry that I wouldn't be able to stop him from going. As we stood at the corner of Logan and Main, Sam pointed toward City Hall.

"Look! Smoke," he gasped.

A thin column of black smoke was climbing into the sky. Almost at once, we heard a sound like firecrackers.

"Did father say there'd be fireworks?" Sam asked me.

Within a few minutes, crowds began running past us, up Main Street.

"You two had better get home," a woman called to us as she rushed past with two children. "This is no time to be out."

Sam and I looked at each other. We sensed the tension of the people who were passing.

"Look!" Sam said, his voice a choked whisper. He pointed to a truck which was heading down the middle of Main Street. Two soldiers sat in the front of an open cab, and two sat in the back with a machine gun on a tripod.

"We'd better go home, Sam," I said, and I grabbed my brother's arm and pulled him toward me. We ran with all our strength back to Sid's house.

Mother was alone in the house. "They've brought in the army," I shouted.

"And they have guns," Sam continued. We could barely catch our breath.

Mother's face turned pale. "Where have you been?" she asked.

We told her what we had seen from Main Street and the dull cracking noises that had come from the direction of City Hall.

I knew that Mother was worrying about father and Sid who were in the demonstration. "We'll just have to wait," was all she said, and she sat down at the kitchen table.

It was late afternoon when father and Sid came home. Father was holding a rag to Sid's head and supporting him as he walked.

"Mother," father called, "get a bowl of warm water and some bandages."

We all sat in the kitchen as mother washed and dressed the gash that ran down the side of Sid's face. "We need a doctor," mother said gravely. "This is too deep for just bandages."

But Sid would not see a doctor and told mother just to use the iodine and sticking plaster that was there. As she finished her work, father began to describe the scene downtown.

"It all got out of hand," he said shaking his head. "Some of the young men set a streetcar on fire right in front of City Hall. People began throwing rocks and bricks. Then the mounties came up the street on their horses. Obviously, the mayor had already decided that that was how he was going to meet the demonstrators. The mounties had their clubs out and began swinging them at people. People began picking up anything that they could use for protection. Then some men tried to pull the mounties off their horses. People started to run in every direction. It seemed as if things were about to explode."

"Good thing, too," Sid murmured.

"Yes," father said angrily. "The third time the mounties came along they had their revolvers drawn."

"Did they shoot?" Sam asked.

"Yes, they shot into the crowd. People must have been killed, but who knows how many."

"Oh, no," mother gasped.

"By then, Sid and I were a fair distance from City Hall, but we ran right into the Specials. They had spread themselves across Main Street to keep people from getting away. I saw Wright, leading one lot. They were like maniacs, hitting everyone in sight with clubs and chasing people down side streets. That's when Sid got hurt."

"He's lucky to be alive," mother said, looking directly at father.

"It's not what we planned when this all began,"

father said at supper: "I had hoped for something better than this after four years in the trenches."

"It'll get better, Ken," mother said. "We've lost this fight but there will be other chances."

"I'm not so sure," was all father replied.

It frightened me to hear father sound so discouraged. I remembered how excited and optimistic he had been only a few weeks before when the streetcar drivers had joined the strike. Was it only a few weeks?

The strike ended officially a couple of days later. Everyone who could went back to work. No one would give father a job because of his work with the strike committee.

One morning, father called Sam and me into the kitchen. Mother was already there.

"Well, children," he said, "we've got to leave Winnipeg. We'll starve if we stay here any longer."

"But where can we go?" Sam cried.

"Sid is helping us get to Ontario. They say there's work there."

"Ontario?" I echoed.

I couldn't leave Winnipeg. It was my home. I would even live on Logan Avenue, but I couldn't leave. I had never said anything to Sarah. Somehow I had hoped that when the strike was over, we could go back to being friends.

ELEVEN

FOR a few days, no one mentioned moving. Sam and I whispered to each other that maybe father had changed his mind. Then, one afternoon, he said, "We have train tickets to Toronto tomorrow. We'll all have to help get things packed and ready by then."

"And to put Sid's house back into the shape it was before we came," mother reminded us. "I hope you children realize just how much Sid has done for us," she went on.

It was the first time I had stopped to think about how long we'd been living with Sid. I hadn't thought about the night we moved for a long time. Sid's house had almost become my home.

"I'm going to say goodbye to Sarah," I told mother.

Mother nodded to me, but said nothing.

I started walking along Logan to Main Street and then back toward my old neighbourhood. I had gone off without saying a word and now I was going back to say goodbye forever. I wondered what Sarah would say.

I was walking more briskly as I turned the corner of our old street. There was our house, still shining white and looking as it had when we left. The door of the house was open and I felt funny when I thought about someone else living there. There was a baby carriage on the walk outside the front door.

Sarah will like that, I thought. We both liked looking after babies, and now she had one living right next door. I reached the Wright's house and stopped, not sure what to do. As I stood there, Gipsy came down the front steps and walked toward me. She was purring and she rubbed her grey fur against my legs. I felt as though she was welcoming me home.

"Did you miss me?" I asked the cat, bending down to stroke her back. As I squatted on the sidewalk, petting Gipsy, I heard voices and laughter in the treehouse. I was about to call when a woman came out of my old house.

"Emily," she called. "Sarah. The lemonade's ready girls."

In a moment, Sarah and another girl came down from the treehouse. The girl was about the same age as me and had long red hair.

"Come on Emily," Sarah called, and they started to skip toward the woman.

"Sarah," I started to call, but my throat was dry and no sound came out.

The girls went into my house and the door closed behind them.

I stood staring for a minute. I felt sad, but I knew I wasn't going to cry. Instead, I just turned and started home. Gipsy followed me for a little while, but soon ran back to hide in the shade of the front porch.

"Goodbye Gipsy," I said. "Goodbye Sarah."

I never saw Sarah again. Perhaps she never knew that we moved.

We left Winnipeg on Friday. Father did find work in Toronto, but it was a long time before things began to go right again.

AFTERWORD

COULD this really be Canada? Troops patrolling the streets. Machine guns at key intersections. Daily battles between workers and police. Labour leaders arrested without charges, imprisoned without trial, their homes broken into without warrants. Canadian citizens rounded up and deported without warning.

Indeed all this — and worse — happened in Canada in 1919. And all because the workers of Winnipeg went out on strike for things we take for granted today: the right to organize a union; to bargain with their bosses; and to earn a living wage.

To achieve these goals, the workers launched a general strike which closed down the entire city.

Nothing — and nobody — worked. Industries were shut down, stores closed, food deliveries cut off. There were no police, no firemen, no trains. Elevators stopped running, telephones went dead, gasoline and coal disappeared, and water became scarce. A modern industrial city had been brought to a shuddering halt by some 20,000 workers who were demanding their rights.

Canada had just emerged from a bloody war leaving 60,000 men lying in European graves. The Communists had overthrown the Russian government of the Czar and were now urging workers throughout the world to stand up to their leaders. Most Canadian soldiers were returning home to find that their jobs had disappeared or been taken by those who had stayed home. Others were sent to Siberia to help restore the Czar to power. Because of the unprecedented wartime inflation, unions all over the country were flexing their muscles and demanding changes.

Industrialists and their friends in government convinced themselves that revolution was at hand. They were determined to crush the Winnipeg Strike and teach workers a lesson they would never forget. Unions would have to be brought in line, before they became too powerful.

Winnipeg was polarized — split down the middle — in one of the great class confrontations in North American history. On one side stood the strikers and their families, some 100,000 strong; on the other, in almost equal numbers, the city establishment and its supporters made up of prominent businessmen, professionals and the like.

It was no contest. Assured of government support, the employers refused to negotiate with the strikers, nor would they accept any compromise. They were determined to destroy the strike, and with it unionism in Winnipeg.

They succeeded. The city police force had been fired for supporting the strike. But with the help of specially chosen deputies, armed with baseball bats and wagon yokes, and of the Royal Canadian Mounted Police, the strike was broken — along with the arms, legs and heads of many strikers. On July 26, 1919, forty-one days after the strike began, the workers admitted defeat. They would return to their jobs and to conditions which were even worse than those existing before May 15 — but many of the jobs no longer existed.

Without question the strike was a disaster for the Winnipeg workers. They had gambled everything on it and had lost. The idealism and energy that fueled Western Canadian radicalism for a decade was spent — quenched by the all-powerful combination of business and government. For the next decade or two little was heard from the labour movement of Western Canada, once the most militant and vibrant in the nation.

Yet the strike was not a total failure. Out of it grew a sense of class solidarity amongst Winnipeg workers which would be translated into votes at election time. Soon the workers of the city were regularly sending labour members to the House of Commons and to the provincial legislature. The battles they had lost on the streets of Winnipeg — for union recognition, collective bargaining and a living wage — would now be fought, and won, in the halls of Parliament.

Fifty years after the strike collapsed — almost to the very day — the workers got their revenge. On June 25, 1969, the people of Winnipeg and of Manitoba went to the polls and put into power a Socialist government consisting of the sons and daughters — in a spiritual, if not a physical sense — of the Winnipeg strikers. Victory was a long time in coming, but it was nonetheless sweet.

Irving Abella
Professor of History
Glendon College
York University